W9-AOZ-629

Dot &
Jabber

and the Great Acorn Mystery

Ellen Stoll Walsh

Green Light Readers

HOUGHTON MIFFLIN HARCOURT

Boston New York

The illustrations in this book are cut-paper collage.
The display type was set in Berkeley Oldstyle Medium.
The text type was set in Berkeley Oldstyle Book.

The Library of Congress has cataloged the hardcover edition as follows:
Walsh, Ellen Stoll.
Dot and Jabber and the great acorn mystery/written and illustrated by
Ellen Stoll Walsh.
p. cm.
Summary: Two mice try to figure out how a little acorn turns into a huge oak tree.
[1. Acorns—Fiction. 2. Oak—Fiction. 3. Mice—Fiction.] 1. Title.
PZ7.W1675Do 2001
[E]—dc21 00-8706

ISBN: 978-0-15-202602-8 hardcover
ISBN: 978-0-544-79164-0 GLR paper over board
ISBN: 978-0-544-79165-7 GLR paperback

Manufactured in Malaysia
TWP 10 9 8 7 6 5 4 3 2 1

4500594154

For Laura, Glenn, Jennifer and Molly Linton,
and Rena Howell—
curiouser and curiouser

The detectives had nothing to do.

"We need a mystery to solve," said Jabber.

"Here's a mystery," said Dot. "What is this little oak tree doing here?"

"Why is that a mystery?" Jabber wanted to know.

"Because of the acorn," said Dot. "How did it get here?"

"Dot," said Jabber, "what acorn?"

"Acorns are oak tree seeds. This little oak tree grew from an acorn, and acorns come from big oak trees."

"Oh, *that* acorn," said Jabber. "But where's the big oak tree?"

"That's part of the mystery," said Dot. "Let's look for clues."

"Okay!" shouted Jabber. "Because we're detectives!" He poked his head into a hole.

"Hey, this is *my* hole," said a mole. "Go away. There are no clues down here. Try the big oak tree—on the *other* side of the meadow."

"Of course!" said Dot. "Come on,
Jabber!"

"That's a long, long way," said Jabber.
"How did our acorn get from there to
here? Do you think it walked?"

"Let's find out," said Dot. "The acorn began at the big oak tree. So will we."

The detectives set off across
the meadow.

After a while Jabber said, "I'm tired. Can we wonder about all these maple seeds instead?"

"There's no mystery in maple seeds," said Dot. "They have wings that twirl, and they ride the wind across the meadow."

"Maybe our acorn rode the wind, too," said Jabber.

"That is what we are going to find out," said Dot.

At last they arrived at the
big oak tree.

"Look!" said Dot. "I bet there are a million acorns here."

"They don't have any wings," said Jabber. "But they taste good."

"Don't eat them, Jabber! They're clues," said Dot.

"Acorns don't have wings, but they might have sneaky feet," said Dot. "Let's keep watch and see if they start to move."

Plip. An acorn dropped from the big oak tree.

Jabber poked it with a stick. "This acorn isn't going anywhere," he said. "None of them are."

A squirrel came and sat down among the acorns.

"Jabber, look!" Dot whispered. "What is he doing?"

"Oh!" gasped Jabber. "He is eating our clue!"

"He can't be," said Dot. "The shell is still on it."

"So why is he stuffing it in his mouth?" asked Jabber.

The squirrel ran off.

"Oh no, he's stealing the acorn!"
the detectives cried, and ran after him.

When the squirrel stopped, they stopped—and watched to see what would happen next.

"What's he doing now?" asked Jabber.

"Digging a hole," said Dot. "Look!
He's hiding the acorn."

Jabber stared at Dot. "Maybe he's
planting it!"

"Of course!" said Dot. "Our acorn crossed the meadow on squirrel feet."

"And got planted by squirrel feet," said Jabber.

"And grew into the little oak tree," said Dot. "The mystery is solved. We are two clever mouse detectives."

"Hurray!" shouted Jabber. "Now what will we do?"

"Find another mystery," said Dot.

"But I'm hungry," said Jabber. "First let's go eat some of those leftover clues."

More About Acorns and Oak Trees

Every full-grown oak tree has acorns, and every acorn is the seed of a new tree. Millions and millions of acorns drop from oak trees every year, and many acorns travel to other locations where they sprout and grow into new trees.

Some acorns travel by squirrel, as Dot and Jabber discovered. Squirrels gather acorns, carry them away, and bury them to store and eat later. If a squirrel doesn't come back for an acorn, the acorn may sprout and grow into an oak tree.

There are many other ways acorns move from place to place. Probably the most common mode of travel is by water. Oak trees growing near lakes, rivers, and streams drop acorns into the water, and the currents carry acorns far from the parent trees. When the acorns wash up on land, some sprout and grow. Birds and other animals may pick up acorns and carry them to new places. People help acorns travel, too, by collecting them and dropping them someplace else.

Did you ever think about what would happen if *all* the acorns from *all* the oak trees sprouted and grew? There would be a lot of oak trees! Luckily, nature keeps everything in balance. Animals eat most of the acorns on the ground, and just enough of the ones left behind grow into oak trees. When the time comes, those new trees drop acorns, and the cycle continues.